For more than forty years,
Yearling has been the leading name
in classic and award-winning literature
for young readers.

Yearling books feature children's
favorite authors and characters,
providing dynamic stories of adventure,
humor, history, mystery, and fantasy.

Trust Yearling paperbacks to entertain,
inspire, and promote the love of reading
in all children.

OTHER YEARLING BOOKS YOU WILL ENJOY

◄ **THE KIDS OF THE POLK STREET SCHOOL**

by Patricia Reilly Giff

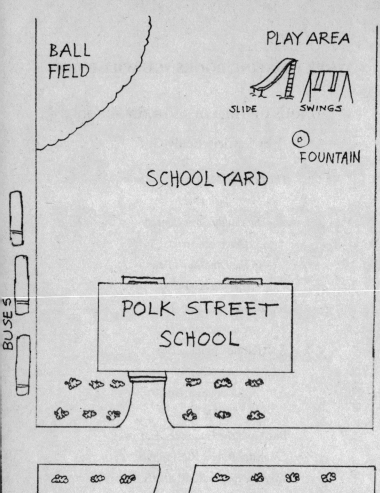

BALL FIELD

PLAY AREA

SLIDE   SWINGS

FOUNTAIN

SCHOOL YARD

BUSES

POLK STREET SCHOOL

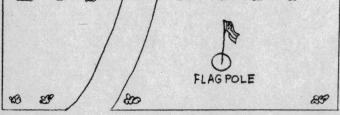

FLAG POLE

...TREET SCHOOL

Emily Arrow Promises to Do Better This Year

Patricia Reilly Giff

Illustrated by Blanche Sims

A YEARLING BOOK

Published by Yearling, an imprint of Random House Children's Books
a division of Random House, Inc., New York

Text copyright © 1990 by Patricia Reilly Giff
Illustrations copyright © 1990 by Blanche Sims

Visit us on the Web! www.randomhouse.com/kids

Educators and librarians, for a variety of teaching tools, visit us at
www.randomhouse.com/teachers

ISBN: 0-440-40369-3

Printed in the United States of America

November 1990

21

OPM

For Carol Geller,
with love

Chapter 1

"Hey," yelled Emily Arrow. She looked around. "I forgot my purse."

Ms. Rooney rolled her eyes. "Hurry. The bus is leaving in a few minutes."

Emily raced back up the path.

Inside the school, a sixth-grade monitor pushed open the door.

"Thanks," Emily said. She headed down the hall for Room 113.

If only her purse were there.

Everything she needed was tucked inside. Her lunch. A dollar for a souvenir. Cookies for a snack.

Today was trip day.

Ms. Rooney's class was going to the museum.

They were going to look at dinosaur bones.

Emily stopped for a quick look at the hall bulletin board.

The first graders had drawn Happy New Year pictures.

They were all scribble-scrabble.

Emily quick-stepped around the corner.

Behind her someone else was hurrying too.

Emily didn't stop though.

"Wait up," a voice yelled.

Emily turned.

It was Dawn Bosco.

Dawn was wearing a pink polka dot hat.

It was a little too big for her. It hung down over one eye.

Dawn wasn't such a hot friend, Emily thought.

Dawn had a pencil with a tassel. She had pink socks with white lace.

Emily clicked her teeth.

That Dawn Bosco thought she had everything.

"Beat you to the classroom," Dawn said.

"What are you doing here?" Emily asked. "I thought everyone was on the bus."

Dawn raised one shoulder in the air. "I forgot my lunch. I think I left it in the closet." She crossed her fingers. "I hope so."

Emily crossed her fingers too.

"Giddap," yelled Dawn.

They raced the last few steps to the door.

Emily reached for the knob and turned it. "Locked," she said.

"Yeow," said Dawn. "We'll have to go to the office for the key."

Emily took a breath.

Suppose they missed the bus.

"Hurry," she yelled.

"Giddap," yelled Dawn again.

They sped down the hall—straight into Mrs. Miller, the substitute teacher.

Mrs. Miller frowned at them. "Go back down the hall and walk," she said.

"But—" Emily began.

"We have to—" Dawn said at the same time.

"No buts," said Mrs. Miller.

They went back to the classroom door and started over again.

Mrs. Miller nodded at them. "Good," she said. "Now you don't look like a pair of horses."

"Neigh," said Dawn under her breath.

Emily started to laugh. Quickly she covered her mouth.

In the office, Mrs. Lee was typing. She looked up as they marched in. "I thought you were going on a trip today," she said.

"We need the classroom key." Emily tried to catch her breath. "Please."

"I think you're going to miss the bus," said Mrs. Lee. She reached for a key on a string. "You'd better fly."

They dashed out of the office. "Flap your wings," said Emily.

"Don't flap too fast," Dawn said. "Mrs. Miller may see you."

They went down the hall, laughing.

"I hope you're good at locks," Emily said at the door. "I'm the worst unlocker in the world."

"Don't worry." Dawn raised her elbows up. She made believe she was flapping.

Then she stuck the key in the lock.

The door opened one, two, three.

Inside, Emily could see her purse.

It was hanging on her chair.

"Thank goodness," she said.

Dawn raced into the closet. "Come to me, peanut butter sandwich," she said. She grabbed her lunch bag.

Then they hurried out of the classroom.

"Will you take the key back?" Dawn asked. "I'm dying for a drink of water."

Emily nodded. She raced for the office.

Behind her she could hear Dawn. "Neigh," she was saying.

"Neigh," Emily yelled back over her shoulder.

Chapter 2

Emily was last on the bus.

Only one seat was left.

She slid in next to Dawn.

"Made it," Dawn said. "Whew."

Emily smiled. "I flapped my wings," she said.

Dawn was turning out to be better than she had thought. Much better.

The bus pulled away.

"Off to the museum," said Ms. Rooney. She was holding on to a pole in front. "What a nice New Year's treat."

Then she clapped her hand to her head. "New Year's," she said. "I completely forgot."

Emily reached into her purse.

Inside was a ham sandwich, a fat apple, and a box of pretzels.

She took out a pretzel for herself and one for Dawn.

"Resolutions," said Ms. Rooney.

Emily looked up. She couldn't remember what they were.

Ms. Rooney looked down the aisle. "Can anyone tell me . . ."

Noah Green's hand shot up.

So did Timothy Barbiero's.

They were smart kids, Emily thought.

She ducked down a little.

She didn't want Ms. Rooney to call on her.

She saw that Dawn was ducking too.

"Neigh," Emily whispered.

Ms. Rooney looked at Noah. "Tell us," she said.

"Rez-o-loo-shuns," Noah said. He stretched out the word. "My father made one. He says he's going to fix up his workroom."

"Yes," said Ms. Rooney. "That's a good one."

Wayne O'Brien raised his hand. "My brother wants to do a hundred push-ups a day."

"Whoo," said Beast. "That's some res-olution."

Ms. Rooney nodded. "Let's pick some too. Make them special. Things you want to do this year."

Dawn handed Emily a pile of raisins.

Emily loved raisins. "How about coming for a sleep-over tomorrow?" she asked Dawn. She tossed a raisin into her mouth. "If my mother says it's all right."

"Great." Dawn tossed a raisin into her mouth too. "I'll ask my mother."

"I can't think of a resolution," Jill Simon called out. She looked as if she were going to cry.

"Who can help?" Ms. Rooney asked.

Linda Lorca raised her hand. "Maybe Jill should have a resolution to stop crying."

"I am not crying," said Jill.

"Just an idea," Linda said.

Emily munched on the raisins.

She couldn't think of a resolution either.

Maybe she could promise to do better this year.

What a stinky resolution.

Besides, she had used the same one last year.

She crossed her fingers. *Please let me think of something,* she told herself.

She saw that Dawn's fingers were crossed too.

"Today is Friday," said Ms. Rooney. "Think hard for the next few days. On Tuesday we'll paint our resolutions on mural paper."

Linda Lorca raised her hand again. "My resolution is to learn all my number facts. I'll write them all over the place."

Tuesday. Emily let out her breath. She had five days to think.

And she was going to think of something better than number facts.

She just hoped she'd have enough time.

Chapter 3

It was Saturday morning. Emily could hear something. She opened one eye.

Clara, Aunt Betty's cat, was awake too. The Arrows were cat-sitting this week.

Pa bom. Pa bom.

Emily opened her other eye. She knew it was her little sister. Stacy had gotten a paddle with a ball on a rubber band for Christmas.

She sighed. Sometimes Stacy was a great kid. Sometimes she was a pain in the neck.

"You give me a headache, Stacy," she said.

Pa bom. Pa bom. "Time to wake up, old Emily," Stacy said.

She was leaning over the bed. "Don't forget the k-u-p-s," she said.

"K-u-p-s?" Emily asked.

Then she sat up straight. Cupcakes.

Tonight Dawn Bosco was coming for a sleep-over.

She had a thousand things to do.

Stacy was dancing around the bedroom. "I love to cook, cook, cook," she sang.

It was a good thing they had bought package-mix cupcakes, Emily thought.

She'd make them one, two, three.

She was going to put piles of icing on top.

Her mother had promised to help.

Stacy was going to help too.

Emily put her feet over the side of the bed.

She had been dreaming of resolutions. "I wish I could think of one," she said out loud.

Stacy stopped dancing. "One what?"

"One resolution," said Emily.

"What's a remolution?" Stacy asked.

Emily looked around for her sneakers. "Resolution."

"Well?" Stacy hopped up to look in the mirror. Clara hopped up too.

"This is a new year," said Emily. "We're supposed to start over."

"All right," said Stacy. "We'll start over." She wrapped her old stuffed snake around her feet. "How?"

Emily looked up at the ceiling. "That's what I'm trying to figure out."

Stacy thought for a minute. "I have one. I'm going to be the prettiest kid in my class."

She smiled, showing all her teeth, even the back ones.

Emily tried not to laugh.

Stacy was as skinny as a string bean.

Her hair was hanging down in front of her eyes.

And when she smiled like that, she looked like Elwood, the dog down the block.

Stacy looked in the mirror. "Do you think I look like a movie star?"

Emily crossed her fingers behind her back. "Almost."

"That's what I thought." Stacy went down the hall to brush her teeth.

Emily stood there grinning for a moment. Then her mother came down the hall.

"Emily Arrow," she said. "Look at this bedroom." Her mother shook her head. "I'll bet Dawn Bosco's doesn't look like this."

Emily sighed.

Junk was all over the room.

There was a hole in her bedspread too.

She had cut it herself when she was making paper dolls last week.

She wondered what Dawn would think.

Her mother was right.

Dawn had the best bedroom in the world.

She got up and opened her closet door.

Then she stopped.

She had the perfect resolution.

This was going to be her perfect year.

She was going to be perfect.

She was going to clean her room, one, two, three.

She was going to study.

She'd end up the smartest kid in the class, the best.

She crawled into her closet and began to throw everything out.

Chapter 4

It was getting dark.

Emily shoved a pair of socks in the hamper. Dawn would be there any minute.

She looked around her bedroom. It was worse than when she had started.

Too bad she had spent most of the day watching cartoons.

Piles of games were all over the floor.

Clothes were on top of her bed.

She shoved the games into the closet.

"What's doing, old Emily?" Stacy

climbed on Emily's bed and sat in the middle of the clothes.

"I'm trying to clean this room," Emily said.

Stacy yawned. "Mother said I can stay up late."

Emily smiled. Stacy would be asleep in no time.

Just then the doorbell rang.

"Dawn's here." Stacy jumped off the bed and ran down the hall.

Emily went through the pile of clothes.

She pulled on her red blouse and started for the stairs.

She looked down.

Dawn Bosco was standing in the hall. She was holding a sleeping bag and her jacket. Clara was rubbing against her legs.

Stacy was standing next to her. She was smiling like that dog, Elwood, again.

Emily clicked her teeth.

21

Dawn's dress was blue. It had a lace collar and diamond buttons.

Emily wondered if the diamonds were real.

Dawn was wearing new shoes too. They were patent leather with the toes poked out.

Emily had never thought about dressing up.

She raced back to her bedroom and looked in the mirror.

Good grief.

She was a mess.

She tore through the pile of clothes on the bed.

She had to find something fast.

Her pink party dress was on the bottom.

It had a dark chocolate stain on the collar.

She pulled on the dress and reached for her Wheat-O pin. It was silver and red, and sparkled in the light.

Her grandmother had gotten it in a Wheat-O cereal box.

Emily pinned it over the stain.

Not so hot for a perfect person, Emily thought.

She pushed her clothes under the bed and went downstairs.

"Hi," Dawn said, smiling. She smoothed down her dress.

Emily saw that Dawn was looking at her collar.

Maybe she could see the chocolate under the Wheat-O pin.

Emily made believe she was shining it with one hand. She made sure the chocolate didn't show.

Emily's mother popped her head out the kitchen door. "New Year's treats," she said.

"Come on." Emily couldn't wait for Dawn to see the table.

She and Stacy had decorated it with brown napkins left over from Thanksgiving.

They had little turkeys on the edges.

She and Stacy had piled the cupcakes they had made on a plate. They looked spectacular.

They went into the kitchen.

Stacy kept jumping around.

She hit the ball with the paddle.

"Watch me, everyone," she said. *Pa bom. Pa bom. Pa bom.* "I'm up to three."

Dawn covered her ears. "You're giving me a headache."

Emily shook her head at Stacy. Sometimes Stacy liked to show off.

Her mother was shaking her head at Stacy too. "Can you girls manage all right?" she asked. "I'm going upstairs to write some Christmas thank-you notes."

Emily nodded. "Sure."

She passed the cupcakes around.

She took a huge bite.

Delicious.

"Let's write resolutions," Dawn said. "Do you have any paper?"

"Sure we do," said Stacy. She yanked open a drawer and pulled out some scrap paper and pencils.

"Good," said Dawn. "Here goes." She reached for a pencil, thinking.

Then she started to write.

She looked up. "How do you spell gorgeous?"

Emily looked up at the light. "G-o-r-g-u-s."

Then she leaned over to watch Dawn write.

BUY A GORGUS NEW SWETER WITH CHRISTMAS MUNEY.

26

"No good," Emily said. "It's supposed to be something like studying hard or—"

Dawn laughed. "This isn't a real resolution. It's just for fun."

Emily clicked her teeth.

She couldn't think of any just-for-fun resolutions.

It had been hard enough to think of a real one.

She picked up her own pencil. PREFECT, she wrote.

She took another bite of her cupcake. "How do you like these?"

Dawn ran her tongue over her lips. "Aren't they from a package mix?"

Emily nodded. "I made them myself."

"My cousin Megan and I made cupcakes last week," Dawn said. "We didn't use a package though. We made the whole thing."

Emily stared at Dawn.

Dawn was turning out not to be so hot.

"My cousin Jessica loves my cup-cakes," Emily said. "She says they're the best. I guess she's my best friend too."

Stacy frowned at Emily.

They hadn't seen Jessica for two summers.

Emily picked up her pencil again.

She curled her hand around the paper so Dawn couldn't see.

EXTRA RESOLUTION:
NEVER INVIT D.B. AGAIN.

Just then, Clara jumped up on the table. She knocked over a glass of water.

It poured over the plates.

The turkey napkins were ruined.

Clara raced across the table. She dived down the other side.

Dawn pushed her chair back. "It's all over my dress."

"Too bad," said Emily. "My cousin Jessica wouldn't mind that. I'll be glad when she comes to see me."

Inside she felt mean.

She was glad Dawn's dress was a mess.

Dawn glared at Emily. "I'm going home," she said. "Right this minute. And you've got a big chocolate stain on your dress."

Then she raced out of the kitchen and went into the hall. She grabbed her jacket and her sleeping bag.

Emily looked after her.

She tried to think of something to say.

Dawn had ruined her sleep-over.

She hoped Dawn got a bunch of snow in her shoes with the stick-out toes.

Chapter 5

It was Sunday afternoon. Emily was sitting on her bed with Clara.

She kept thinking about the fight with Dawn.

Dawn had been such fun in school.

At home she was no fun. No fun at all.

Forget Dawn Bosco for a friend.

Emily shook her head. That sleep-over had been some mess.

Dawn had run down the street in the dark.

Emily's father had to go out without his jacket. He had to walk Dawn home.

Emily had ended up getting the blame for the whole thing.

She punched up her pillow.

Tomorrow was a spelling bee.

Dawn was one of the best spellers in the class.

Too bad.

Emily was going to be perfect.

She was going to win that spelling bee if it was the last thing she did.

"Monday," she said to herself. "M-u-n-d-a-y."

She took a look at her spelling book. "M-o-n . . ." she said.

She hated spelling. H-a-t-e-d.

She walked her feet up the wall. "Tuesday," she said. "The hardest one of all.

"T . . ." she began, "e-u . . ."

She sneaked a look at the spelling book. Good grief. It was u-e.

She looked at the ceiling. "T-u-e. T-u-e. I'll never remember."

She rolled off the bed onto the floor.

She was going to stay up here all day. She'd stay for a hundred hours if she had to.

That was her stinky resolution for today. Otherwise she was going to turn out to be the worst speller in the class.

She looked up at the ceiling.

She couldn't stand it anymore.

If she didn't breathe some nice snowy air, she'd scream.

She sat up.

That's what she'd do. Just go outside for a little bit.

When she got back, she'd learn her spelling words one, two, three.

She grabbed her jacket and boots.

She pounded down the stairs.

Stacy looked up from the television.

"Put on your jacket, Stacy," Emily said. "Let's go."

Stacy smiled with all her teeth. She slid off the couch.

Outside, a few minutes later, they went down the street together.

"Where are you going?" Stacy asked.

Emily looked around. "How about the schoolyard? Always piles of snow there."

They started to run.

Behind the gates, Beast was jumping on the pile with Matthew.

Timothy Barbiero was there too.

"Come on, Emily Pemily," Beast yelled.

Emily raced to the top of the pile with Stacy.

The snow was smooth and hard.

She slid down in back of Beast.

She went like the wind.

"Yeow," she yelled.

She sat at the bottom for a moment.

It was a great day.

She climbed to the top again.

Timothy slid next.

Then Stacy.

"Hey," said Beast. "How about a war?" His face was red from the cold. So were his hands.

Emily was a little cold too. She wished she had remembered her mittens. She smiled. "Great. A war."

"Me and Beast . . ." Matthew began. "Against—"

"Boys against girls," Timothy Barbiero said.

"Yeah," said Beast. "Good."

"No good," said Emily. "Stacy's too little to—"

"I am not," said Stacy.

"You can have Dawn Bosco too," said Matthew. "Here she comes."

Emily looked across the schoolyard. Dawn was jumping across the snow piles.

She was wearing a new scarf with fringe.

Emily put her hands on her hips. That Dawn Bosco was always there to ruin everything.

"Hurry up, Dawn," Matthew yelled. "You and Emily and Stacy against us guys."

Emily looked across at the boys.

She could see Beast was packing a snowball. "Wait a minute," she called. "Time. I'm not—"

Whoosh!

Beast's snowball missed her by an inch.

"You don't even know how to aim," she yelled.

She scooped up a snowball and threw it as hard as she could.

Beast ducked away from it. "Get them, men," he yelled.

A moment later, Matthew and Timothy started to throw snowballs too.

"Hey," yelled Dawn Bosco. "Give me—"

"Hey," Emily yelled too. "Dawn's not on my—"

Beast didn't stop. He threw another snowball.

Emily reached for another clump of snow.

She raised her arm back and threw it as hard as she could.

She wished she were throwing it at Dawn.

The snowball sailed up high. It smashed into Beast's face.

"Hey," he yelled.

"Too hard," Matthew shouted.

Beast stood up. He ran his sleeve across his eyes.

Then he jumped over the fort and started down the street for home.

Emily stood there for a moment.

She couldn't believe it.

Beast was crying.

"It's all your fault," she told Dawn Bosco.

She swallowed. "Come on, Stacy," she said. "I think we'd better go home too."

Chapter 6

It was Monday morning. Emily walked to school slowly.

She tried to think of what to say to Beast.

Maybe he wouldn't even talk to her.

She went into the classroom and started for the closet.

Beast was jumping around at the coat hooks.

She stopped for a minute. Maybe she should say she was sorry.

She opened her mouth.

He tapped her on the arm. "Emily Pemily," he said, and grinned.

Emily blinked. "Beast Feast," she said.

She went into the closet.

Beast had forgotten all about it.

What a good friend he was.

She frowned.

Dawn Bosco's coat was hanging from the hook Emily always used.

Emily marched all the way down to the end of the closet.

She piled her jacket and hat on a hook.

The jacket was too puffy. It slid down to the floor.

That happened every day. So what! The jacket was so old her wrists were hanging out.

She straightened her collar with the Wheat-O pin.

Sherri Dent came along. "This closet is a mess," she said. "Junk all over the floor."

Emily started to make a face.

Then Sherri smiled. "I'm going to pick everything up."

She reached for Emily's jacket. "That's my resolution."

Emily changed her face.

She smiled back.

Sherri stuck Emily's hat on top of the shelf. "Only on Mondays. I don't want to be in here forever."

She looked at Emily's Wheat-O pin. "Nice."

"From my grandmother," Emily said.

Up in front Ms. Rooney clapped her hands. "How many think they're good spellers?"

Emily went back to her seat.

She took a last look at her spelling book.

If only she had studied harder yesterday instead of going out.

Next to her Dawn was writing in her diary.

I LOVE A SPELLING BEE.

What a show-off that Dawn was.

"Ready. Set. Go," said Ms. Rooney.

Everyone raced to the sides of the room. Girls on the window side, boys on the door side.

Emily raced last.

She was glad Beast and Matthew were worse spellers than she was. They'd be out ahead of her.

They always were.

"Spell *Monday*," Ms. Rooney told Linda Lorca.

Everyone pointed to the chalkboard.

Monday, January 6, was up on top.

"Oops," said Ms. Rooney. "How about *Friday*?"

"Easy," said Linda. She spelled *Friday* so fast Emily couldn't keep up with her.

Emily crossed her fingers. If only she didn't get *Tuesday*.

She tried to spell it in her head.

"*West,*" Ms. Rooney asked Matthew. "I can't believe it," Matthew said. "I know that one. W-e-s-t."

Emily poked her head out of the line.

It was almost her turn.

She could feel her hands getting wet.

She took a deep breath.

Just then the door opened.

Mrs. Gates, the third-grade teacher, popped her head in.

Mrs. Gates was Ms. Rooney's best friend.

"Happy New Year," she told everyone.

"Happy New Year," everyone yelled back.

"Do you all have wonderful resolutions?" she asked.

"I've got mine," said Timothy.

"Me too," said Sherri Dent.

"How about you?" Mrs. Gates asked Ms. Rooney.

Emily was surprised that Mrs. Gates would ask. Ms. Rooney was really perfect. She didn't need resolutions.

Ms. Rooney looked serious though. She nodded at Mrs. Gates. "I'm going to be a better teacher this year."

Mrs. Gates smiled. "That's my resolution too."

She waved at the class.

Then she went out the door again.

Ms. Rooney looked at Jill. *"Friend."*

Emily crossed her fingers for Jill.

Jill knew it though.

It was Beast's turn. *"Beg,"* said Ms. Rooney.

"Whoa," said Beast. He made believe he was wiping his forehead. "That's easy. B-e-g."

Then it was Emily's turn.

"Tuesday," said Ms. Rooney.

Emily closed her eyes. *Was it* T-e-u *or* T-u-e?

She wiped her hands on her jeans. "T," she said slowly. She started over. "T-u-e."

Right, she told herself. "T-u-e-d-a-y," she said as fast as she could.

Someone in front of the line said, "Too bad."

Ms. Rooney shook her head. "Sorry, Emily."

"Tuesday," said Dawn. "Easy. T-u-e-s-d-a-y."

Emily swallowed. She had forgotten the *s.* The easiest thing in the world.

She went back to her seat.

She was the only one sitting in the whole classroom.

She took out a piece of drawing paper.

She bent her head down a little so no one would see she was almost crying.

She blinked hard.

No, she wasn't crying.

She was angry. Angry at everything.

Most of all at know-it-all Dawn Bosco.

Chapter 7

School was over for the day.

On the way home Emily jumped over the snow piles with Stacy.

They climbed their front steps.

Emily reached for her key.

It was hanging around her neck on a sneaker lace.

"Hurry," Stacy said. She jumped up and down. "I'm freezing to an icicle."

Emily yanked on the string. "Here it is."

It reminded her of something.

What was it?

Then she remembered.

Dawn Bosco.

She and Dawn laughing. Dawn flapping her arms as she opened the classroom door.

Emily put the key in the lock.

She turned it, and turned it again.

"Can't you ever do that right?" Stacy asked.

Emily felt the lock click.

A moment later they were inside.

Everything was so quiet Emily could hear the faucet. Water was dripping into the kitchen sink.

She shivered a little.

She hated it when her mother wasn't home.

Stacy looked up at her. "I'm glad you're here, old Emily."

"Nothing to be afraid of." Emily crossed her fingers. "Mommy will be home from the dentist soon."

Emily threw her coat on the chair.

She went into the kitchen. Clara was asleep on the table.

Emily looked for the peanut butter jar.

Stacy followed her into the kitchen. "I can't eat anything. Not one little thing."

"I can," said Emily. "I could eat a whole elephant, even the ears."

"We had a Happy January party today." Stacy slid onto a chair. "We had to tell something nice about someone. We had food too."

"Nice." Emily pulled out the box of saltines.

She wished she were in kindergarten again.

She wouldn't have to worry about mean people like Dawn Bosco.

She wouldn't have to worry about being the worst speller in the whole United States.

"No," said Stacy. "It wasn't nice at all. The food was yuck-o." She frowned. "So was the tell-something-nice part."

Emily smeared a pile of peanut butter on the cracker and took a bite.

She gave a piece to Clara too.

She thought about Dawn again. "Come to me, peanut butter sandwich," she had said.

Stacy kicked the table leg. She looked as if she were going to cry.

Clara jumped down. She curled around Emily's feet.

"What's the matter?" Emily asked.

"I'm not telling," Stacy said.

Emily ate around the edge of the cracker. "Then I'm not telling you my secret when I get one."

Stacy looked up. "Really?"

Emily smiled. "No, not really. Tell me what's wrong."

Stacy kicked the edge of the table again. "My New Year's resolution is no good."

Emily tried to think. She couldn't even remember what Stacy's resolution was.

"I was going to be the prettiest kid in the class," Stacy said.

"You're pretty." Emily tried to get the peanut butter off the roof of her mouth with her tongue.

Stacy shook her head. "A.J. said I look like a dog when I smile."

Emily thought about Elwood, the dog down the street.

"That wasn't very nice of him," she said slowly. "But being pretty isn't the important thing anyway."

Stacy looked out the window. "I told you my resolution was no good."

Emily could see Stacy had tears in her eyes. She slid a cracker across the table. "Eat this. You'll feel better."

Stacy took a bite of the cracker. "Put a little more peanut butter on the next one," she said.

Emily reached for the cracker box.

"I don't know why A.J. said that anyway," Stacy said. She raised one shoulder. "I told something nice about him."

Emily sat up. "What did you say?"

"I said he had a nice long neck. Nice and smooth like a noodle."

"Oh." Emily leaned back against the chair. She tried not to laugh. "Maybe A.J. doesn't like having a noodle neck."

Stacy looked at her. "Why not? I wouldn't mind."

"I think you hurt his feelings."

Stacy thought for a minute. "He hurt mine too."

"But you hurt his first."

Stacy looked up at the ceiling. "I guess that's right."

"Maybe you could call him on the phone," Emily said. "Maybe you could say you're sorry."

Stacy thought for a minute. "Maybe. I know his whole phone number by heart. It's the easiest in the world. 555-1111."

Stacy reached for the phone. "You're a good sister," she said.

Emily took the last cracker. She listened as Stacy punched the buttons.

"Hey, Emily," Stacy said. She covered the receiver. "Why don't you call Dawn Bosco? Tell her you lied about Jessica. Tell her Jessica's not your best friend."

Jessica? For a moment Emily didn't know what Stacy was talking about.

Then she remembered. She had told Dawn that lie about Jessica Saturday night.

She shook her head. "That's different."

She put the cracker down. Suddenly she didn't want it anymore.

Chapter 8

Today Emily wore her father's old shirt.

She wore her worst jeans, with the spot on the knee.

She didn't care.

Everyone was supposed to dress in paint clothes.

Even Ms. Rooney was wearing a warm-up suit with paint dots.

Besides, Emily thought, she had something else to worry about.

It was Tuesday. The class was going to paint a New Year's resolution mural.

Ms. Rooney was going to hang it in the cafeteria.

The whole school was going to see it.

Emily swallowed. How could she write that she was going to be perfect?

She couldn't even spell *Tuesday*.

She thought about her bedroom.

That was still a mess too.

Next to her, Dawn was working on a math sheet.

She covered it quickly when she saw Emily watching.

Quickly Emily looked away.

Everything was going wrong this year.

"Line up, everyone," Ms. Rooney called. She picked up a package of mural paper.

Everyone went out the door.

Emily went last.

She saw Stacy and A.J. marching down the hall with the milk money.

Stacy was talking a mile a minute.

She looked happy.

Emily looked at Dawn.

She wished Dawn had phoned her to say she was sorry.

Out in the hall, everyone stood back.

Ms. Rooney began to roll out the paper.

It spread past Mrs. Gates's room, down the hall, almost to the office.

"Now we're set," said Ms. Rooney.

In back, Beast and Matthew were fooling around, laughing.

Ms. Rooney raised one eyebrow.

Beast gave Matthew a push.

Matthew landed on the paper.

He left a sneaker print right in the middle.

Ms. Rooney clapped her hand to her head. "I might as well get a job in the circus."

Everybody laughed, even Emily.

Beast was a funny boy.

He didn't stay angry at a person forever.

Like that snowball fight!

Too bad Dawn wasn't like Beast.

Everyone took a spot in front of the paper.

Emily was stuck between Beast and Dawn.

Too bad.

Beast was the best artist in the class. And Dawn was hogging up the whole space.

Emily sat back.

She tried to think of a great resolution.

She looked up at the wall.

Everyone else was painting.

Just then Matthew yelled, "Watch out."

Jill Simon jumped back. "Oh, no."

Beast jumped back too. He started to laugh.

A jar of red paint was rolling down the mural paper.

Red paint was splashing over everything:

the paper, the wall, Jill Simon's paint clothes, Beast's picture.

"Sorry," yelled Matthew.

"I don't believe he did that," Ms. Rooney said. "Someone get some paper towels."

Emily jumped up. "I'll go."

She raced into the classroom.

She headed for the closet.

No towels.

Yes, one. It had been stepped on though.

She dashed out the door again. "Sorry," she told Ms. Rooney.

"Good grief," said Ms. Rooney. "Go quickly. Get the key from Mrs. Lee. Get some from the supply room."

Emily started down the hall.

"Take someone with you, if you like," Ms. Rooney called.

Emily turned.

Dawn was staring at her.

Emily shook her head. "I can go alone," she told Ms. Rooney.

She looked back at Dawn again.

Dawn looked as if she were going to cry.

Chapter 9

No one was in the office.

Emily looked around.

The supply room key was on Mrs. Lee's desk.

She wondered if she could just take it.

Ms. Rooney was in a big hurry.

By now there'd be red paint all over the hall.

Just then, Mrs. Lee poked her head up from behind her desk.

Emily blinked.

"I'm looking for my comfortable shoes," said Mrs. Lee.

"May I take the key?" Emily asked. "I have to hurry. I have to get—"

Mrs. Lee waved her hand. "Go right ahead."

She disappeared under her desk again.

Emily dashed down the stairs.

She stopped at the bottom.

Which way?

She turned to the right and stopped at the supply room door.

Why had Dawn looked so sad?

Emily swallowed. She felt sad too.

She wished she hadn't said that stuff about her silly cousin Jessica.

She wished she had picked Dawn to come with her.

"Emily Arrow," she told herself aloud, "you're turning into a mean kid."

She looked around. She hoped no one had heard her.

She put the key in the lock.

Suppose it didn't open?

She could go upstairs.

She could ask Dawn.

The key turned easily.

It would have been nice to have Dawn Bosco for a friend again, she thought.

She grabbed a roll of paper towels and started up the stairs.

"Hurry," Ms. Rooney was calling as she reached the top.

Emily put on a burst of speed.

She could see a fat path of red down the middle of the mural paper.

Jill Simon was crying. She was shaking her hands up and down. "There's paint on my father's best paint shirt."

Matthew and Beast were jumping over the paper.

Red footprints were caught along the edge.

Emily gave Ms. Rooney the supply closet key. Then she tore off towels to mop everything up.

Dawn grabbed a few. So did Sherri and Linda.

Beast ran for the wastepaper basket.

In two minutes it was filled to the top with a mess of red paper towels.

Then Ms. Rooney rolled out new paper. "Let's be more careful," she said. "Let's get this job done right."

Emily rubbed her hands on her paint shirt.

She picked up a brush.

She looked at Dawn out of the corner of her eye.

"I haven't seen my cousin Jessica in a long time," she said.

Dawn didn't answer.

"I don't even remember what she looks like."

Dawn dipped her brush into the yellow paint. "Sometimes I make cupcakes from a box," she told Emily. "They're just as good."

Emily nodded. "Almost."

She leaned over. "I was afraid I wouldn't get the lock to open," she said. "I should have taken you with me."

Dawn started to paint a yellow sun. "I'm a good door unlocker," she said.

"Yes," Emily said.

Dawn splashed some blue paint around her sun. "You've got to get a good sky." She cleared her throat. "That's a great pin. You always have the best stuff."

"Me?" Emily said, surprised. "I have good stuff?" She ran her fingers over the Wheat-O pin.

Then she leaned over. "Want to be friends?"

Dawn smiled. She dipped her brush into the paint again.

She started to draw two girls.

One had a big blob of paint on her shoulder.

Dawn was a messy painter.

As messy as Emily.

Emily cleared her throat. "What's your picture about?"

Dawn looked down at her paper. "My resolution."

Emily wanted to ask what it was.

She didn't though.

Emily drew a round circle.

"What are you painting?" Dawn asked.

"A girl. Me." Emily painted in a neck. "I've got the same old resolution as last year. Emily Arrow promises to do better."

She smiled a little. "Is that you?" She pointed to one of the girls on the paper.

Dawn nodded. "Right."

"You made a mess out of the other girl," Emily said. "All that paint on her shoulder."

Dawn looked surprised. "It's a pin. Just like yours."

Emily worked on her painting for a few minutes.

She felt wonderful inside.

She knew Dawn's resolution had to do with being friends.

It was going to be great to be friends again.

She really was going to do better this year. Better in school. Better with Dawn Bosco.

She was going to begin right now.

She reached up and took her Wheat-O pin off her shirt.

She tapped Dawn on the shoulder.

"Here," she said. "This is for you."

"Wow." Dawn smiled. "It's the best."

Another thing she was going to do, Emily thought. She was going to call her grandmother tonight. She was going to ask her to get another box of Wheat-O right away.